# Porridge the Tartan Cat and the Unfair Funfair

Written by Alan Dapré

Illustrated by Yuliya Somina

Young Kelpies

THIS BRAW BOOK BELONGS TO

## Porridge the Tartan Cat

Pat ma paws and
you can read it too.

# 1

# A Few Words

Hi, it's me.

I'm Porridge – the world's only tartan cat.

6

Everyone knows I toppled into a tin of tartan paint when I was wee. So I am not going to say any more about it. I am *not* going to tell you that I toppled into a tin of tartan paint and became  from top to toe.

## 🐾 Me-oops 🐾

I just did.

I *ever-so-very-much* want to tell you all about my latest tartan tale.

I've just got to finish my fishy biscuits first.

## 🐾 Me-crunch! 🐾

I want to become big and strong like the McFun twins, Isla and Ross. They like eating lots of greens and oranges and other tasty colours. We need to eat so we have plenty of energy to go on our Porridgy adventures – especially Roaring Ross in this fangtastic story!

Today we're off to the **FangFair**. It's a wee bit dark and spooky so you might want to read with the light on. (It'll help you see the words.)

If you're so scared you need to look at something warm and fluffy, I'll be curled up in the corner.

It's time for my catnap.

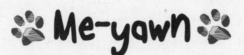 **Me-yawn**

Read on... if you dare!

# 2
# You Dared!

Once upon a newspaper, there was a tartan cat.

Me!

(It's a cat thing.)

"Off you get, Porridge," said Mum. "I want to put that newspaper in your litter tray."

 Me-leap! 

"Hold on, let's keep this one," said Dad, quickly picking the paper up.

"Why?" asked Ross and Isla, the twins.

"Look." Dad showed them the **Tattiebogle Bugle**. "Porridge wasn't the only one on the front page."

"Dad! That's you!" shouted Ross.

Isla read the story aloud: "Local Tattiebogle archaeologist Mr McFun believes a stinky space rock crash-landed in the grounds of Tattiebogle Castle four-hundred years ago."

## 🐾 Me-wow! 🐾

"How did you find that out?" asked Ross.

"Archaeologists don't just dig in the dust," replied Dad. "I was digging around in the library and found an old book about the castle. It said a rock fell to earth and there was a terrible smell of stinky sprouts! A pong so strong that people who smelt it were knocked out for a week!"

## 🐾 Me-whiff! 🐾

"My guess is the rock was made of

# SPROUTINIUM,"

said Mum, who is a scientist. "Sproutinium is the smelliest element in the universe. Always keep away from smelly old rocks."

"And Dad's smelly old socks," giggled the twins.

"I'd love to do a dig in the Tattiebogle Castle grounds," said Dad, "but a funfair has just arrived and the owner won't let me near it."

"Is it the **FANGFAIR**!?" Ross and Isla whooped in their clever-together way. (It's a twin thing.) "Wahooo! It's here at last!!"

"What's a **FANGFAIR**?" asked Mum.

Ross pulled a crumpled leaflet from his pocket.

"Can we go?" asked Isla.

"Aye," said Dad. "Maybe I can do some space-rock snooping while you two have fun."

*Och, there's nothing fun about a funfair. I once got stuck inside a—*

"Hey, Porridge," said Ross, with a cheeky grin. "Remember when you got stuck inside a squeaky candyfloss machine because you thought there must be a wee mouse in it?"

*How could I forget?*

I had jumped in.

## 🐾 Me-spin! 🐾

Then I'd whirled around, and came out covered in pink fluffy stuff! The twins said I looked sweet. I tasted sweet too. It took me a week to lick off all that icky sticky candyfloss.

# ❧ Me-yuck! ❧

And I never did find that squeaky mouse.

## Mmmm. Mouse.

# 3

# Fishy

##  Me-squish!

Isla sat on a tartan cushion. Then she realised it was me! "Sorry, Porridge! What are you doing here?" she said in surprise and a car.

*I've just come along for the ride,* I meowed. I didn't want to miss out on the **FangFair** adventure. (It's a curious cat thing.)

"Och, you might as well come," chuckled Dad.

By the time we reached the **FangFair** at the big ruined castle, a huge cloud had covered the sky and darkness had fallen (then picked itself up and pretended nothing had happened). A million rides twinkled and swung and clattered and spun and *I am not exaggerating.*

"Seven rides and three stalls," counted Ross.

*OK, maybe just a wee bit.*

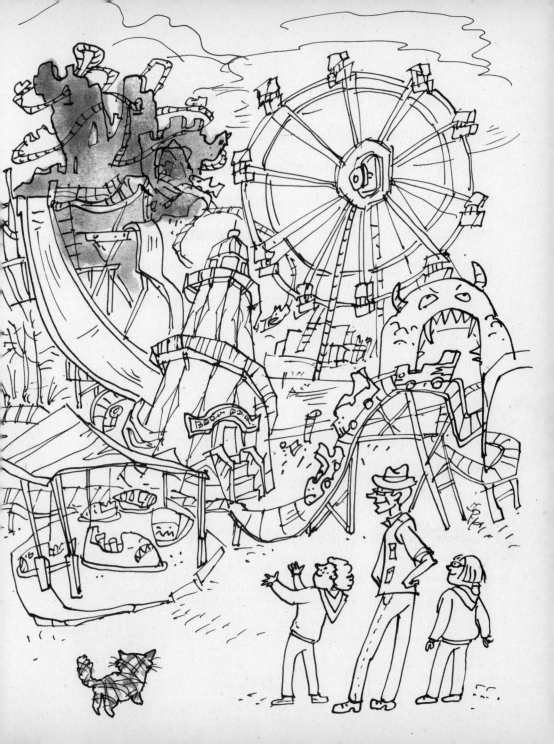

"There's no one here." Isla glanced around the funfair-filled grounds of Tattiebogle Castle. "It's empty!"

"Well, at least you won't have to queue," said Dad. He stretched out on a bench and yawned. "I'm going to wait here and rest and see if I spot any space-rock clues while you three have fun. Let me know if you smell anything sprouty and suspiciouzzzzZZZZZZZZZZZZZZZZZZZZ..."

"That was quick," said Isla.

"He's fast asleep!" said Ross

*Aye, really fast!*

While Dad had a *quick* nap we strolled to the nearest stall, where there was a shallow pool of water behind a wee wooden barrier. Sad, dusty toys sat on some shelves nearby, and a wonky sign read:

Hook a **PERILOUS** piranha to win a **TERRIFYING** toy prize!

I hopped onto the barrier and keeked into the pool.

It was full of toothy fish!

## Mmmm. Fish.

Ross saw me licking my lips. "These piranhas aren't real, Porridge. They're made of wax!"

Suddenly someone stepped out from the shadows, making me jump!

## 🐾 Me-jump 🐾

"Welcome to my FANGFAIR," said a man with a crooked grin. *And a crooked wig.* It looked as if he'd stuck a stack of old birds' nests on his head.

## Mmmm. Birds.

"Try your luck." He handed Ross a crooked rod with a crooked hook on one end. (It all looked a bit crooked to me.) Ross leaned over the barrier and held out the rod, but it was too short to reach the pool. (I told you it was crooked.)

"Porridge, give me a helping hand, I mean paw," said Ross. "You're brawsome at catching fish."

"It's a cat thing," said Isla.

*Hey, that's my line!*

Ross picked me up and put the rod between my front paws. When he held me out, I was *ever-so-very* close to the pool. And I hooked a piranha!

# 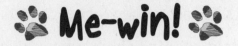 Me-win!

"Which prize will you pick?" asked Isla.

"I'll have that **ScareSoaker** please," said Ross, pointing to a toy that could squirt out water.

"No!" grunted the **FangFair** owner. "You and that cat were very clever but you don't get a prize. You broke two rules."

He pointed to a tiny sign:

RULE 1: NO CATS ALLOWED.

RULE 2: SEE RULE 1.

"But that's unfair," said Ross.

"It's an unfair funfair," sniggered the owner.

"He thinks he owns the place," grumbled Isla.

"I do," he said, waving them away with a crooked finger. "Off you go. That moth-eaten moggy is getting up my nose— **CAT-CHOOOO!**"

We scampered away to explore a bit more.

"Let's find some things that go bump in the night!" said Isla.

"Spooky ghosts?"

"No, dodgem cars!"

# 4
# Dodgy

Two children and a tartan cat (me) stood by the dodgem car ride. It looked about as much fun as a trip to the vet.

"It's just a rickety shack where cars go smack," rhymed Ross.

The twins chose a blue dodgem car and squeezed in like sardines.

## Mmmm. Sardines.

I clung to a tall pole on the back and we waited for the ride to start. All of a sudden, nothing happened.

Then a bit more nothing.

Suddenly something *did* happen! The **FangFair** owner climbed into a red dodgem car. I recognised his crooked grin and his crooked wig. And the crooked way he was staring straight at us. He was driving straight at us too! Sparks showered down from the pole at the back of his car.

"Let's get going!" urged Isla.

"I can't reach the pedal," cried Ross. "This dodgem car is dodgy!"

"Hold on, Porridge," yelled Isla. "There's going to be a big..."

# BUMP!

We spun and spun. It wasn't fun. I dropped dizzily onto the foot pedal, bashing it down with ma big bahookie.

"You did it, Porridge!" boomed Ross, as we whooshed forward. "Let's bump that car back!"

Ross spun the other car out of the dodgem shack... and I was flung onto Isla's lap.

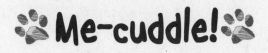

The unfair funfair owner stormed over with a terrible face like thunder (and a terrible simile too because thunder is just a sound).

"This is *my* dodgem ride. I'm meant to be doing all the bumping," he said, doing all the grumping instead. "And I told you to get rid of that tartan cat! It's time I went and found Nibbles."

I licked my lips.

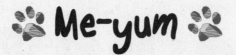

## 🐾 Me-yum 🐾

"I don't think he means wee tasty treats, Porridge," whispered Isla.

"Aye. Nibbles is my pet wolf! She'd love to nibble some *Porridge*."

## 🐾 Me-gulp 🐾

He blasted out another sneeze. This one was bigger than before, with more O's.

# CAT-CHOOOOOOOOOOO!

It gave me a such a chill, I nearly jumped out of my tartan coat.

I ran off through the **FangFair**, not knowing where my frightened legs would take me.

# 5

# Stinky Drink

My legs took me into Chapter 5 and stopped by a tall tower with a round bell on the top. It was a tatty Frankenstein-themed test-your-strength machine.

My *mega-super-well-OK-not-bad* ears heard frantic footsteps.

"Phew. We thought we'd lost you," said Ross, running up. "That would have been a **CAT**astrophe!"

*Hey, I do the cat jokes around here*, I meowed.

"This looks fun," puffed Isla. "You have to swing

a big hammer to ring a bell."

Weary after all that running, I sat down heavily and...

# CLANGGGGG!

...sent the bell soaring towards the end of this story.

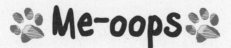 **Me-oops**

"Wow! Your furry bahookie just set a new world record!" laughed Ross.

The excited twins were **itching** to explore the

# FangFair.

*scratch* Whenever I mention **itching** I start
*scratch* to get all **itchy** and have *scratch* to have
a good old — What's the word? *scratch*

Aye, that's it.

Are you **itchy** yet?

## Scratch!

"Can anyone see a really scary ride?" asked Ross.

I pointed a trembling claw at a watery ride called

# Dreich Creek.

Dripping WET boats were dashing down a WET
river and splashing over a WET waterfall.

*I don't want to be a SOGGY MOGGY!* I yowled.

"It's OK, Porridge," said Isla. "We won't go on that one."

"Let's try *this* creepy ride instead!" shouted Ross,
running towards...

The rusty **HowlerCoaster** track wound around Tattiebogle Castle itself. It looped and swooped though the windows and doorways, with more twists and turns than school-dinner spaghetti.

A drawbridge clattered down and something scary howled into view!

## 🐾 Me-help! 🐾

"It's just an empty carriage," said Ross, as it shuddered to a stop beside us. I cheered up when I spied the number 13 on the side. That's my lucky number. (I can cram 13 fishy biscuits in my mouth in one go.)

## 🐾 Me-yum! 🐾

The unfair funfair owner shuffled towards us, with his crooked wig swaying like a wobbly haystack.

## 🐾 Me-groan 🐾

Just in time, I jumped in the carriage and pretended to be fluffy tartan cushion. He snorted suspiciously, then grunted to the twins, "I'm glad you got rid of that irritating **TARTAN** cat. Have a ride on this **HowlerCoaster**. And a drink too." He handed them both a crooked bottle of **ScareJuice**. "Only drink it when you see the sign. And look out for scarewolves."

"What's a scarewolf?" asked Ross.

"It's a mythical mash-up of werewolf and wulver," explained the owner in a low voice. "Werewolves are people who become wolves; they're fierce and nimble.

Wulvers are half wolf, half human. They love fish and are very good at sniffing out smelly missing objects."

## Mmmm. Fish.

As he walked off to a kiosk, the twins crammed into the carriage with me in the middle.

"Don't worry, Porridge," said Ross. "Everything on the ride is fake and not what it seems."

"Aye, it's bound to be fishy," agreed Isla.

## Mmmm. More fish.

Our carriage began to rattle along the rusty rails and take us into castle! That was when my *mega-super-well-OK-not-bad* eyes spied a hairy wolf! A real live wolf! Not a wax one or a cuddly toy! What did the **FangFair** owner say his pet was called?

# NIBBLES!

The wolf licked her lips as if I was one of the Three Little Pigs!

 Me-gulp!

She looked at me, and licked her lips again.

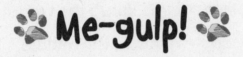 Me-gulp

**NIBBLES** wanted...

# NIBBLES!

# 6

# On A Roll

Fortunately, carriage 13 set off, trundling away from Nibbles into the crumbling castle. It rumbled past a model of a scarewolf, fishing in the moat.

"So *that's* a scarewolf..." said Ross. "It doesn't look very real."

"Aye, it's just a mechanical monster," agreed Isla.

I knew it wasn't real, but I flicked out my claws in full *mega-super-well-OK-not-bad-ninja-cat* mode. I was ready for anything the ride could throw at me.

# SLAPPP!

A wet fish landed in my lap.

🐾 Me-yum! 🐾

"I told you this ride would be fishy!" giggled Isla.

I gave the fish a cheeky lick.

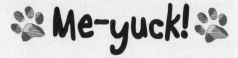 **Me-yuck!**

It was made of wax!

We clattered through the castle kitchen and swung under an archway into the **Ye Olde Dining Hall**. A painting hung on the wall of a dug with a ruff going (ruff). We trundled by a table full of tasty-looking food.

I sneakily chomped on a chicken leg.

Wax.

I munched a mackerel.

Wax.

A candle.

Wax.

# 🐾 Me-yuck-yuck-yuck! 🐾

"Silly old Porridge. Nothing is real, remember?"
chuckled Ross.

I practised my yowling as we trundled along:

*We left the fake kitchen and rumbled outside,*
*Up up up up on a heart-thumping ride,*
*Whooshing through windows and swooshing*
*through holes,*
*Swooping and looping with breathtaking rolls,*
*We whizzed halfway up then we started to drop...*
*Down down down down down!*
*To a wheel-sparking stop!*

## 🐾 Me-phew 🐾

Our carriage was now in a creepy courtyard, surrounded by swirling mist and shadowy figures. And an iffy whiffy fishy smell...

"This courtyard stinks of rotten seafood," Ross coughed.

The terrible pong was ever so strong!

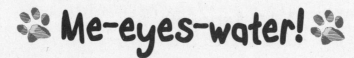 **Me-eyes-water!**

A sign read:

# NOW IT'S TIME TO ENJOY YOUR DRINK. PLEASE WOLF IT DOWN.

"Purr-fect timing, eh Porridge?" gasped Ross. "I need a drink after all that **HowlerCoaster**ing."

"Me too," agreed Isla.

The thirsty twins quickly flipped open their bottles. Big bouncy bubbles bobbled out and burst on my *mega-super-well-OK-not-bad* nose.

# 🐾 Me-sniff! 🐾

The **ScareJuice** smelt very fishy to me. But not in a good way, like salmon or trout. It smelt wrong, like the fishy pong in the misty courtyard.

*Don't drink it!* I meowed, sensing danger and trouble for the twins. I leapt off the carriage seat – in *mega-super-well-OK-not-bad-ninja-cat* mode – and pawed Isla's bottle onto the track. Then I acrobatically batted Ross's bottle!

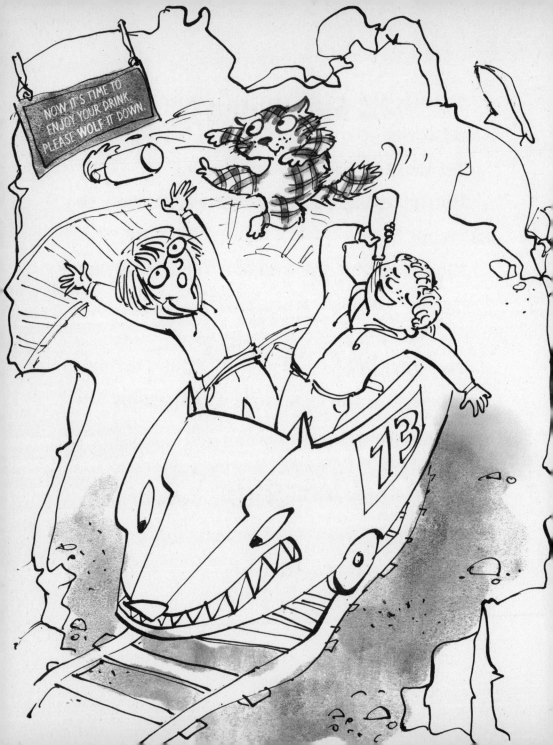

#  Me-swipe

Too late. Ross had drunk every drop.

"What's wrong, Porridge?" said Isla. "You're acting very odd."

"Och, *I* feel a bit odd," said Ross, rubbing his belly. Suddenly the sign swung up.

And right in front of us stood the FangFair owner, with nasty Nibbles by his side.

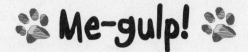

# 7

# Tattieburgle Town

Quick as a tartan flash, I pretended to be a cushion again. The **FangFair** owner was grinning. His wolf was whining. She could smell cat – even though I'd washed behind my ears this morning.

"Shush now, Nibbles," snapped her owner, beaming at the twins. "It's time I introduced myself properly. I'm Fangus McFungus. The meanest triplet in all of Tattiebogle Town. And Scotland. And the world. And that twinkly stuff up there."

My *mega-super-well-OK-not-bad* eyes glimpsed

a wee label on his wonky wig.

Then I glimpsed a tattoo on his arm.

Aye, it was Fangus McFungus all right.

The name was known to every scaredy cat in town. No one dared meow his name aloud. Instead, it was whispered. Or mimed very badly. Fangus McFungus was no fan of cats. Not since the day a cat sat under his wig to keep out of the rain, thinking it was a bush. Fangus sneezed that cat into next week, poor thing. He had a **CAT**-astrophic cat allergy.

"We've met your brother and sister," said Ross.

Fangus raised a hairy eyebrow in surprise.
"Really? Then you'll know ma brother Fergus wants
to rule the world. And Windy Wendy wants a cat the
colour of that tartan cushion. As for me? Och, I just
want to steal things and become disgustingly rich!"

He rubbed his hands together greedily, then
rubbed his crooked nose, which had become red and
itchy. "Are you sure you got rid of that cat?"

"I can't see a cat," Isla said, truthfully.

# 🐾 (Me-cushion) 🐾

"I need you two clever kids to help me," urged
not-to-be-trusted Fangus. "I read in the newspaper
that a smelly space rock once crash-landed by
Tattiebogle Castle. I plan to sniff it out and create

a really big stink across the whole town! One whiff of it, and everyone will be sleeping like babies – even the babies. Then, while they're snoozing, I'll take whatever I please. Gems, jewellery, antique furniture, some toilet rolls because I'm running out…"

"**We won't help you**," said Ross, boldly.

"You will, once that **ScareJuice** has turned you both into scarewolves."

The moon peeped out curiously from behind a cloud, and bathed the creepy courtyard in a pale blue light.

"Ross, look at your hands!" gasped Isla.

"This is scary – they're turning hairy!" Ross spluttered.

"You'll soon be a mega-whiffy, ultra-sniffy scarewolf," cackled Fangus. "Then you're going to sniff out the stinky space rock with my other

scarewolves and help me bogle all of Tattieburgle.
I mean burgle all of Tattiebogle."

"Noooooooooo!" howled Ross, and he leapt out of
the carriage.

What happened next was beastly. I'll yowl it for
you:

> Ross sprouted a snout
> And whiskers too,
> His teeth became fangs
> And big paws grew,
> His eyes became orange
> No longer blue,
> He howled at the moon
> Like scary wolves do!

# GRAAGGHH!

*Aarggghh!* I roared back, reusing the same letters because it's good to recycle.

"It's Roaring Ross," chuckled Fangus. "When I blow this whistle he will do whatever I command!"

# Schweeeeeeep

Fangus blew the whistle. Isla heard nothing, but I heard a horrid high-pitched instruction.

Naturally, I ignored it. No one tells us cats what to do! But Roaring Ross sprang forward and stood as still as a scary, hairy statue.

 **Me-gulp!**

# 8
# Rabbiting On

The **HowlerCoaster** still reeked of rotten fish. I'll tell you this for free: scarewolves might smell *really well* with their noses, but they smell *really bad* to everyone else's noses.

## Me-whiff

"Hmmm." Fangus glared at Isla. "You should be a scarewolf by now too."

"I spilt my drink," said Isla, pointing to a puddle

by the carriage. "Now change Roaring Ross back! You're being really stinky. And he's really stinky too! And why aren't there any other visitors at your **FANGFAIR**? What have you done with them?" she asked. These were very good questions (but not as good as "Porridge, would you like some fishy biscuits?")

"I've turned them all into scarewolves. And it's time for you to join them," boomed Fangus, rubbing his itchy nose. He held up another bottle of **SCAREJUICE**. Suddenly, a cushion became a cat and I gave the bottle a sneaky squeeze. Startled, Fangus let out a squeaky sneeze!

# SQUACHOOOOOOO!

"Nice one, Porridge," said Isla as the **ScareJuice** squirted harmlessly onto the floor.

Fangus blew his whistle.

# Schweeeeeeep-peeep-peeep

And Roaring Ross roared!

# GRAAAAGGHHHHH!

More scarewolves appeared and joined in, and soon they were wailing and moving in time together, like a hairy boy band. They all crouched down and looked up and howled at the moon.

The moon took the hint and disappeared quickly behind a cloud. Now everything was nearly as dark as the letters on this page.

"Follow me, Porridge," whispered Isla, darting past Roaring Ross into the the castle ruins.

What else could I do? (Well, I could buy a box of fishy biscuits. Pour out a box of fishy biscuits. Eat a box of fishy biscuits. Buy another box of fishy biscuits. Pour out another box of fishy biscuits. Eat another box of fishy biscuits. Buy another box...)

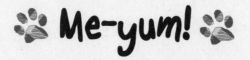

## Me-yum!

Och, forget fishy biscuits – I needed to run after Isla! This was no time for standing there like a frightened rabbit. This was time for running like a frightened rabbit and escaping like a frightened rabbit and hopping into the next chapter like a frightened rabbit.

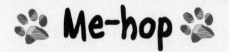

## Me-hop

# 9
# One Good Turn

Of course, one wee hop doesn't get you very far.

Fiendish Fangus was on my tail!

## 🐾 Me-ouch 🐾

*Really* on my tail!!!

Time for a quick getaway! **TURN THE PAGE!** ⟶

**HURRY!**

# 10

# You Did It!

## 🐾 Me-sigh 🐾

Thanks to your nimble fingers, I freed myself from furious Fangus and ran after Isla. I dashed faster and faster, just like you're speeding through this su**PURR**b story! (Don't you worry, there are still plenty of exciting chapters left. Here's one coming up now.)

# 11

# The Workshop

When I stopped running I was bathed in a ghostly green light in a strange room high in the castle. All around me tubes spun, flasks twirled, pans bubbled, wheels whirled and pipes hissed (but not as well as I do).

There was no sign of Isla.

"I'm over here, Porridge," a small voice whispered from under a cobwebbed worktop.

*Isla!* I meowed, happily hurrying to find her.

"I think this could be Fangus's laboratory."
She scratched my head thoughtfully. "What do
you think?"

*It's really stinky!* I hissed.

We crept over to a stack of whiffy bottles.

"I can see **SCAREJUICE** bubbling inside them," said Isla, keeping her distance (and her cat) away from it. "I bet this lab is where Fangus McFungus makes his monstrous mixture. Let's see if there's an antidote, so we can change Roaring Ross back."

We searched up and down. I did the down bits because I'm nearer the ground. After lots of picking things up and putting them back, my curious paws found something incredible.

"Porridge, put down that ball of string," sighed Isla.

## 🐾 Me-play 🐾

Then Isla found an empty cardboard box, which soon became full of Porridge. (It's a cat thing.) After I'd torn it into hamster bedding, we came across a photo of an old lady standing next to Fangus. Someone had drawn an arrow pointing to his crooked wig.

"Who is she?" Isla turned the photo over. *Aunty Dot* was scribbled on the back.

*There was no antidote. Just Aunty Dot.*

Och well.

Without any warning, things began clinking. A carriage was coming up from the direction of the creepy courtyard! Soon two glowing wolf eyes lit up the track. *Was it Nibbles? We ducked...*

## Mmmm. Duck.

...behind a worktop, just as carriage 13 clattered through the cluttered green room.

"There's Roaring Ross," whispered Isla. Her beastly brother was sitting next to Fangus, while the other scarewolves clung on bravely behind.

"It's time I put you pongy scarewolves to work!" cried Fangus. "I want to find that stinky space rock tonight, and rob all the houses in Tattiebogle Town."

With that, he stuffed two sprouts up his nose to block out the scarewolves' disgustingly fishy whiff. Then, with an awful laugh and a rotten wig, they rode off around a corner and were gone.

"After them!" shouted Isla, as carriage 14 rumbled into the lab.

When I saw the empty seat, I knew just what to do.

## 🐾 Me-jump! 🐾

# 12

# The Hole Truth

My four feet flew four feet onto the seat. *What a feat.*

Isla leapt in beside me. "Great thinking, Porridge. With any luck this carriage will take us back out. Let's buckle up and enjoy the ride."

*Enjoy the ride?*

HERE IS A WEE LIST OF THINGS I WOULD ENJOY MORE:

    a) fishy biscuits

    b) biscuity fish

    c) anything to do with fish and biscuits

We rolled away from the loopy laboratory and gratefully left the green gloom behind. I felt the cool night air waggle my whiskers as we corkscrewed up a twisty track, **CLACK-LACK-A-LACK-LACK**, that wound around the old castle. It got whizzy.

## 🐾 Me-dizzy 🐾

"I can see Roaring Ross and Fangus down there," exclaimed Isla, as we rose ever higher on the rails. Roaring Ross and Fangus were still in Carriage 13, slowly approaching the end of the **HowlerCoaster** with the other scarewolves hanging on behind. Fangus leaned out, pushed a lever and a section of track in front of him shunted sideways.

## **CLONK-SHUNK**

"They're going off the rails," gasped Isla.

She was right.

Carriage 13 flew through the air, clattered onto the grass and bounced and bobbled on beyond the unfair funfair. We heard Fangus's far-off whistle...

## Schweeep

...and saw the scarewolves claw the ground. The carriage slowed down, and rolled to a stop by a watery loch. Fangus wasted no time. A second blow of the whistle started the search for the buried space rock. Roaring Ross and the rest of the scarewolves ran off, sniffing and scrabbling and licking things (which was a bit disgusting).

## 🐾 Me-yuck 🐾

In carriage 14, we wound around, high off the ground.

# CLACK-LACK-A-LACK-LACK

"We need to work out where the space rock fell," said Isla urgently.

Aye, I meowed, enjoying my bird's-eye view of the castle.

## Mmmm. Birds.

Suddenly I spotted something strange with my
*mega-super-well-OK-not-bad* eyes. Two round holes
in the ruined castle walls. The bright moon beamed
down through them and onto the loch.

#  Me-eureka!

That space rock Dad read about must have punched two holes through the walls on its way to Earth four hundred years ago, and then landed in the loch – just where the moonlight was landing now!

As we stopped at the top of a very steep drop, I pawed Isla, keen to tell her my news. All she heard was my mews.

"Sorry, Porridge. I don't understand you," she said.

*I* do, growled a deep voice right behind me.

I spun round and saw...

## NIBBLES!

# 13

# Off The Rails

Nibbles was clinging on – and swinging on – the back of our carriage.

*Fangus told me to follow you. I'm glad I did. Now I can show him where the space rock splash-landed,* she growled.

Me and my big (but brawsome) mouth.

The yellow-fanged wolf grinned, looking ready to launch. *And lunch!*

## Me-gulp

But before nasty Nibbles could nibble some tasty Porridge, the carriage screeched downwards and picked up speed. I screeched down too... at a hundred yowls an hour!

Me-yowwww!

"Hold on!" cried Isla, as we rolled off the rails and bounced across the bumpy grass. The carriage careered through the **FangFair**, and sent lots of things flying – especially the birds.

## Mmmm. Birds.

"Hold on, Porridge, something's up..." yelled Isla.

# KA-THUMP

*It's us!*

We hit a big bump and soared into the sky. And when the carriage landed, its four rusty old wheels broke off.

# SPLANG-FLANG-BLANG-CLANG

Now it slid like a sledge towards the loch!

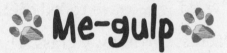 Me-gulp

*Loch out for the look*, I yowled, metting byself in a mit of a guddle.

Nibbles unhooked her claws and howled, *I'm off!*

*Aye, she did whiff a bit.* In one bound, she was on the ground. It was the end of the ride for the stinky wolf.

The carriage came to a sudden stop in the horrid **WET** loch.

"It's OK, Porridge," said Isla. "It floats like a boat."

## 🐾 Me-phew 🐾

As we bobbed on the water, Nibbles loped off to find Fangus. That sneaky wolf knew where the space rock had landed and was off to tell her nasty master! The two stinkers were planning to pong out the town!

# 14

# Hide And Seek

Isla took off her shoes and socks and scooped me up in her arms. Then she bravely stepped into the DEEP water. It went all the way up to her ankles. *I told you it was deep!* She splashed to the shore and put her socks and shoes on her feet, because that was the best place for them.

Hiding behind a tree, we saw Nibbles trotting towards Fangus in the distance. Hold out your thumb as far as you can. That's how big Fangus McFungus would look to you. *And me* (if I had a thumb).

Fangus was blowing his whistle and strolling about as if he was the world's best football referee. His eager scarewolves scratched at the grass and tore up paths, tipped over tubs and ripped up shrubs. Some sniffed. Some whiffed. Some huffed, some puffed. And did lots of other rhyming stuff.

"Where's Roaring Ross?" whispered Isla.

Good question. I hadn't seen him since Chapter 12. Maybe Roaring Ross had found an antidote? Maybe you'll find out if you turn the page?

Maybe not. Ross had found us and he was still

Roaring. Hold your nose! I'll yowl to tell you how bad

he smells:

*Think of kippers and stinky seals,*

*Mouldy prawns and reeking eels.*

*Whiffy whales in salty brine,*

*Jellyfish and sea slug slime.*

*Stir until you rot the spoon –*

*Take a sniff and leave the room!*

He stepped closer, claws glinting, eyes squinting

in the bright moonlight. He was supposed to grab

us, but his paws paused, as if he didn't want to!

Before the boy-wolf could do anything beastly,

the whistle blew.

# Schweeeeeeep

He scampered off to join Fangus and the other scarewolves. Nibbles was there too, pawing at his pesky owner. Fangus's crooked face was growing angry and his crooked wig was, um, not growing at all, because it was a wig.

"What is it, Nibbles?" he shouted. "I need to find that space rock fast! I don't have all night."

*Search the loch!* howled Nibbles.

"I don't understand what you're saying," snapped Fangus, pointing his whistle at the wailing wolf. Nibbles snatched the whistle from her master's hand, took a deep breath and blew.

## Schweeeep

It was a new command, just for Roaring Ross. The beastly boy-wolf hopped, skipped and jumped into the loch (he was so fast he would have won a gold medal

if he had been doing the triple jump in the Olympics
instead of just trying to find a stinky old rock).

Fangus still wasn't sure what was going on.
"What is that scarewolf up to?"

*His ankles*, I muttered.

We watched him scarewolfy-paddle to the spot
where the moon lit the loch, then reach under the

shimmering surface. Would Roaring Ross be the one to find the space rock?

We crept closer to get a better view, trying to stay hidden from Fangus. Isla's feet made no sound on the grass. My feet made no sound on the grass... but LOTS OF SOUNDS ON SOME TWIGS INSTEAD!

SNAP! SNAP! SNAP!

SNAP! SNAP!

🐾 Me-oops 🐾

# 15

# Hold Your Nose!

When the twigs snapped, Fangus snapped too.

"Och, not you two again! Don't move! Whatever that scarewolf brings out of the loch is MINE!"

"I'm guessing that the stinky rock is in the loch," Isla whispered to me.

Aye, I meowed. *I tried to tell you that on page 75.*

If only humans were clever enough to speak Cat. I pointed my tartan tail at the round holes in the ruined castle. The moon shone through them like a torch, lighting up the water. Finally Isla understood. "Ohhh! The space rock must have bashed through the castle and splash-landed in this loch!" she said, a little too loudly.

"You're right!" cackled Fangus, dancing with Joy (one of his scarewolves). "I'm glad I thought of that!"

Och, it was me! Then my *mega-super-well-OK-not-bad* eyes spied Ross sploshing out of the yucky water, clutching something between his paws.

Isla held her nose just in case it was something stinky from Sprouter Space. Don't forget to hold yours again too. (I can't hold my nose because I don't have thumbs.)

Roaring Ross jumped, skipped and hopped his way back to Nibbles. Then he stood as still as someone who is really good at musical statues.

"Show me what's in your paws," cried Fangus.

Roaring Ross didn't move. Fangus snatched his whistle from Nibbles and blew hard.

# Schweeeeeeep

Roaring Ross opened his paws to reveal a wee rock. It was green and round and looked just like the sprouts that Fangus had stuffed up his nose in Chapter 11. The slightest breeze made it glow brighter, and we could just begin to smell its perilous pong.

Then Fangus gently dropped it in a wee glass vial, and popped on a stopper. "This vial will smell vile after a while. It's a good job I've got these sprouts up ma nose. One whiff will knock out everyone in Tattiebogle Town for a week!"

"We have to grab that vile vial," whispered Isla.

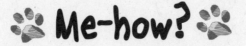 **Me-how?**

I needed some time to think of a plan. So it
would help if you could please turn this page over
really s-l-o-w-l-y.

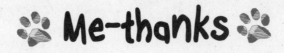 **Me-thanks**

# 16

# Porridge Has A Plan
## (But It's Not Very Good)

Because of your super s-l-o-w page turning, I had exactly the right amount of time to work out how to snatch the vile vial from Fangus.

My plan was simple. All it needed was this:

a) me

b) some running

c) some pouncing

d) more me.

It was so simple it couldn't fail.

*Here goes.*

I ran towards Fangus in my *mega-super-well-OK-not-bad-ninja-cat* mode and... tripped over my tail.

## 🐾 Me-splat 🐾

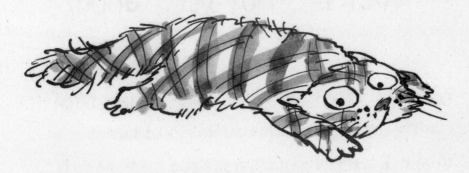

"Drat that tatty cat!" grumbled Fangus, so furious and angry he was **FANGRY**! He blew his whistle and a scarewolf scooped me in its arms. It really whiffed, and ma poor whiskers shrivelled like dried-up worms.

### 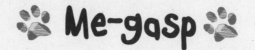 Me-gasp

"I'll save you, Porridge," said Isla, in full
*mega-super-well-OK-not-bad-for-a-human-saving-
Porridge* mode. She dashed across the grass to rescue
me (and hopefully reward me with a fishy biscuit
for being so brave). Isla hadn't gone far, just half a
sentence, when she tripped over a scarewolf's tail.

### 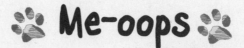 Me-oops

The stinky old scarewolf snatched Isla in a
bear hug (even though it was not a scarebear).
Now there was no way we could retrieve that
rock from Fangus.

###  Me-sigh

*Sometimes things don't go to plan, especially plans.*

"We're wasting time," snapped Fangus, now so furious and grumpy he was **FRUMPY**, which was not a good fashion look. He whistled an order:

# Schweeeep-peep-peep-peep...peep!

All the scarewolves scampered after him. I had no idea where we were being taken. It was a mystery more mysterious than THE MYSTERY OF THE MISSING FISHY-BISCUIT-FLAVOURED ICE CREAM by Conan Flake, my favourite author.

I was about to ask you to flick forward a few pages to find the answer, when Fangus saved you the trouble. "We're going to the giant spinny thing over there."

"It's called the Big Wheel," said Isla.

*Because it's wheely big*, I meowed.

# 17

# Runny Porridge

The scarewolves took us to the big wheel called the
Big Wheel. Alongside it was the wee kiosk that
controlled the ride, called The Wee Kiosk That
Controlled The Ride.

"Time to get the Big Wheel moving," said Fangus,
stepping inside, with terrible mischief in his eyes
and horrid sprouts up his nose. My *mega-super-
well-OK-not-bad* eyes saw a rusty lever on a dusty
control box.

Fangus lifted the lever halfway up. It pointed to FAST so the wheel would go, um, FAST.

"That should be enough," he puffed. The Big Wheel began turning. It would take a few pages to reach the right speed.

"Why are you spinning this ride?" cried Isla. "No one is on it."

"I'm a big fan of this wheel," Fangus bellowed, "and it's a big FAN of mine. When I climb the Helter Skelter and hold up the stinky space rock, this whirling wheel will blow a sprouty smell all over Tattiebogle Town! Then my scarewolves will rob every house. Only after that will I set you and that tatty cat free. Here's something for you while you wait."

"There's always a catch with your giveaways," groaned Isla.

"Aye," said Fangus, throwing her a bottle of **ScareJuice**. "Catch!"

Isla didn't catch it. Instead, she swung her left leg and booted the bothersome bottle into the darkness.

"Bah. I can easily make more," grunted Fangus, nodding at Nibbles. "All I have to do is gather water from my pet wolf's paw prints."

"Is that all?" asked Isla curiously.

"Well, the watery wolf prints must be bathed in moonlight. But that's not really important right now!"

*Wrong.*

*That* was the most marvell-ificen-tabulous-ly essential information in the whole porridgyverse. It gave me a notion how to make my own potion!

"We have to do something," whispered Isla.

*I'm a bit tied up at the moment,* I meowed, still trapped and wrapped in an itchy scarewolf hug, hoping it didn't have fleas.

 **Me-scratch**

I needed to get away.

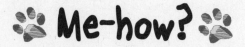 **Me-how?**

"What is that cat scratching and me-howing about?" grumbled Fangus. The nosy nuisance took a step closer to me. THAT was a big mistake. His face crinkled up like an old crisp packet. He wiped his nosy, runny nose on his sleeve and let out a tremendous sneeze –

**CAT-CHOOOOOOO!**

- that blew my scarewolf off his feet. I wriggled free.

"Run!" cried Isla.

I darted off, more runny than Fangus's nose, and quickly hid behind the HOOK-A-PIRANHA stall. I needed a new plan.

## 🐾 Me-think! 🐾

# 18

# The Potion Notion

Just after this chapter started, I had the most fabul-ificent-tastic idea a cat could *ever* have.

## 🐾 Me-eureka! 🐾

I wasn't going to make **ScareJuice** – I was going to make something much better: **PorridgeJuice**! And I had to do it before the Big Wheel reached its full speed...

The ground around the **Hook-a-Piranha** stall

was muddy and damp – I had splashed a lot of water when I fished for a piranha. So now I padded around, leaving deep paw prints in the wet ground.

SQUELCH SQUELCH
SQUELCH SQUELCH

Next I did a very brave thing. I dived into the **Hook-a-Piranha** stall pool like a daft dug. (Don't tell *anyone*.)

# Spa-looooosh!

Wet stuff went everywhere! One very soggy moggy (me) dropped onto the grass, and checked out the porridge prints. They were full of water that magically rippled in the moonlight.

I'd made watery **PorridgeJuice**!

## 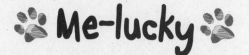 Me-lucky

Next, I picked up the prize prize: a squirty **ScareSoaker**. It would be **PURR**-fect for sucking up the **PorridgeJuice**.

## ✿ Me-sucky ✿

Just then, I saw a wolf print. This one still had a paw in it. And a leg and a body and a tail and if you put that all together you get...

## ✿ Me-tremble ✿

*Fangus told me to follow you!* she growled, with a wolfish grin. *We thought you might try to make some* **SCAREJUICE**. *Then turn him into a scarewolf. Then blow a whistle and command him to stop being naughty. Then get him to open a shop in the Highlands and sell fridge magnets and tea-towels with pictures of tartan YOU on the front.*

I said nothing. I wasn't going to admit I was making **PorridgeJuice**, which would be way better than **ScareJuice**.

Nibbles stepped closer in the howling wind. *I'm here to chase you out of Tattiebogle Town. Or order you a taxi. Once you leave, you can never come back!*

With that, she sprang at me with her claws out!

## 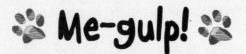 Me-gulp!

Luckily, mid-leap, a blustery gust from the whirling Big Wheel suddenly swirled her away...

*I'll be baaaack*, she howled, because that's what baddies always say.

## 🐾 Me-phew! 🐾

Apart from Nibbles blowing off, which sounds rude but isn't really, things were not looking good. (Except me. I always look good.)

1) Isla was still trapped by a scarewolf!

2) Ross still *was* a scarewolf!!

3) Fangus was about to stink out the town!!!

The Big Wheel was spinning faster and faster –
I had to hurry!

I dipped the **SCARESOAKER** into each Porridgy
pawprint and sucked up every drop of
**PORRIDGEJUICE**.

# SCHHLOOOP

Now I had what I needed to foil Fangus
McFungus. All I had to do was squirt him with
my magical muddy moggy mixture.

Wish me luck...

# 19
# Full of Wind

I stuffed the **ScareSoaker** in my fur coat, and began to bravely battle back through the blustery blasts.

Meanwhile, Fangus was busy climbing the twisty steps of the Helter Skelter as fast as he could, which was *ever-so-really* slow because he never did any exercise – apart from running a tap, or jogging his memory.

Ten minutes later, Fangus reached the top. He was completely puffed out, like that wolf in the three little pigs story.

By now, the Big Wheel was spinning as fast as a hurricane, and blowing as fast as a hurricane, but it wasn't actually a hurricane because it was made of metal and gears and 'stay in your seat' signs.

"When I – PUFF – get ma breath back," gasped Fangus, "I will blow ma – WHEEZE – whistle and order Roaring Ross to yank the lever up to SUPER FAST

speed. Then I'll un-stopper this space rock vial and
– PANT – Tattiebogle Town will be under ma
terrible spell."

Terrible smell, *more like.*

So nothing happened for another ten minutes while everyone waited for Fangus to get his breath back.

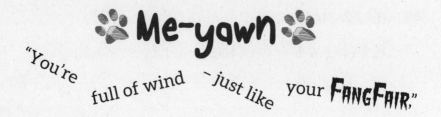

Isla yelled up at him. Her words were being blown about all over the page.

"Your cat may have escaped, but you won't!" he yelled down.

Fangus looked over at her beastly brother. He whistled once and Roaring Ross walked slowly towards the wee kiosk, which was now shaking wildly in the wind. But before he could step inside, it was gone.

# SWOOOOOOSSSHHH

It was blown into the stormy sky just like that wooden house in *The Wizard Of Some-Place-That-Sounds-Like-Australia.*

Luckily for Fangus, the lever for speeding up the ride was left behind.

## 🐾 Me-groan 🐾

The FangFair owner put the whistle to his lips...

# Schweeep-peeeeep

...and commanded Roaring Ross to push the lever to SUPER FAST.

Even though Isla wasn't all there in the Height Department, she was fully grown in the Bravery Department. And the Say-What-You-Really-Think Department. And also the Better-Try-To-Stop-

My-Brother-From-Doing-Something-Daft Department.

"Rosssssssssss! Don't touch that lever or I'll tell Dad!" she shouted.

But the beastly boy-wolf couldn't hear. His eyes were glazed (like the yucky cherries that children pick off cakes, so they can just eat the icing and the sponge bit). He walked like a mummy and a zombie mixed together – a mumbie!

Or was it a zommy?

And began to pull the lever towards SUPER FAST!

It was time to put my **PorridgeJuice** plan into action. As silent and slippery as a cat burglar in slippers, I made my way towards the Helter Skelter slide. No one saw me.

"Hi Porridge," said Isla.

OK. Isla saw me.

As soon as she spotted the **ScareSoaker** in my mouth, she realised I was plotting something. "Are you going to squirt Fangus?"

I nodded, but I had no time to chat. Instead, I scampered up the Helter Skelter slide in slow-motion – because it was really blowy, remember – and it took a really long sentence to reach the top of the twisty steps and meet face-to-leg with Fangus, who held the vile vial in his hand.

*Stay where you are!* I meowed, pointing the

**SCARESOAKER** at him.

Fangus gasped. "Are you going to turn me into

scarewolf?"

*No, a scarecat!*

I squirted his gawping mouth with my muddy

moggy mixture.

"Blurgghhh," he spluttered, as it fizzed down his

throat. "That tasted furrible."

*Zoweee-woweee-meoweeeeee*

And here's a song about what happened next.

*Fangus sprouted a tail*
*And whiskers too,*
*His face became furry*
*And tartan paws grew,*

His ears became pointy
He let out a mew,
Then yowled in the night
Like tartan cats do!

## YOWW-WOWW-WOWWWL

"Wa-hoooo! You're half-man, half-kitten!" shouted Isla, watching from below.

You're a

I meowed.

## 20

# What A Blow

"Bah! I can easily change myself back. I made an antidote with the help of my Aunty Dot!" said furry Fangus, straightening his wonky wig. "It's kept **out of reach** and **surrounded by locks**."

He'd understood me, being half cat, but I could barely hear him. The Big Wheel was now spinning at SUPER FAST speed. A swirly whirly twirly blur!

The **PURR**-fect speed to stink out the town.

#  Me-frown

The tall Helter Skelter wobbled wildly in the wind, more battered than a deep-fried chocolate bar. Fangus held out the vile vial. A stinky green mist was swirling inside.

"If you think being a mitten will stop me, you're wrong! This is the purr-fect mewment to release the pong! Three, two—

That, by the way, was the biggest sneeze in this story. It came from furry Fangus, who was suddenly

sneezing all over the place, but mainly in this book.
He pawed at his fur and he clawed at his tail, and let
out a wail. "What's happening to me?"

"You're allergic to yourself!" whooped Isla.

Furry Fangus yowled with rage.

# YOW-WOWW-WOWWWL

He wasn't the only one furry and full of fury.
Nibbles was back! The wolf was battling step-by-step
against the wind that had blown her away. She had
anger in her eyes, and hedgehogs on her paws (for grip).

*I'm looking for a cat*, she howled.

I ducked out of sight.

## Mmmm. Duck.

Nibbles stared up and saw furry Fangus. The wolf licked her lips. Porridge wasn't on the menu any more!

## 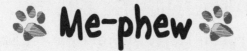 Me-phew

Nibbles swept up the steps, and did a bit of light dusting with her tail. At the top, she paused her paws and stared at furry Fangus, who quivered with fright.

*Go away! Shoo!* he wheezed, in half-Cat language. Then he sneezed again.

For a moment, his eyes were shut. (That *always* happens when you sneeze.) This was my chance to be a hero and grab the vile vial. I sprang like a tartan panther and swiped my paw at the glowing glass bottle.

*Missed*, Fangus hissed, stepping to one side.

🐾 **Me-oops** 🐾

To my surprise, I slid down the Helter Skelter!

🐾 **Me-swooo**

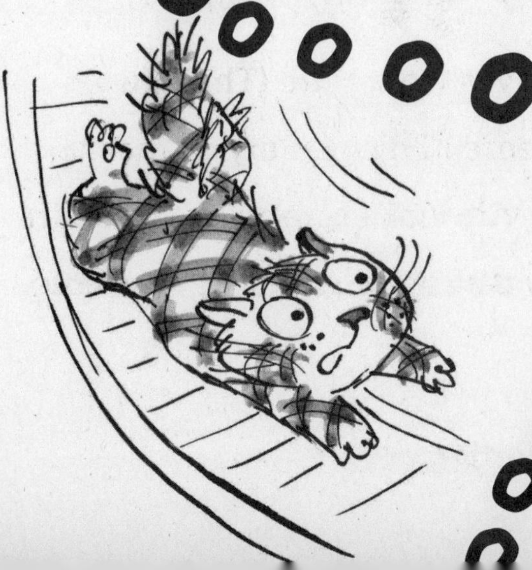

SSOOOOO
SSSSSShh

I bounced at the bottom - on my bottom - and

landed with a

**FLUMMMMPFF**

in a candyfloss machine!

# 🐾 Me-not again! 🐾

Och, I couldn't believe it. I was covered from my nose to my toes in icky sticky candyfloss!

## 🐾 Me-yuck! 🐾

## 🐾 Me-STUCK! 🐾

# 21
# Saved By The Belly

Now, we really needed to stop the Big Wheel, but Roaring Ross was still as still as a statue. Isla was in the grip of a stinky scarewolf. And I was stuck in a sticky candyfloss machine. *Again.*

## 🐾 Me-sigh 🐾

Soon Fangus would open the vile vial and stink out **EVERYTHING!** including the pages of this book. If we didn't stop him you'd never want to read this smelly story ever again!

Only something **TOTALLY** amazing and **SLIGHTY** unbelievable can save us now.

# WHEEEEEEE...

Suddenly the big metal bell from the test-your-strength machine fell from the sky! All the way from Chapter 5.

**TOTALLY** amazingly and **SLIGHTLY** unbelievably, it **BASHED** the Big Wheel lever back down to its OFF position. The wheely Big Wheel slowed. The wind dropped. And everything stopped.

"Saved by the bell," joked Isla.

"**NOOOOOOOOOOOOOO!**" cried furry Fangus using up lots of ink. He leaned out of the Helter Skelter for a better look – and that was when Nibbles bit him on the bahookie!

**OW-WOWW-WOWWW-WOWWWW!**

The beastly baddy threw his mitteny paws in the air... and the vile vial slipped from his furry grip. It was sure to **CRASH** on the ground below and **RELEASE** its awful aroma. We hadn't been saved by the bell, after all...

# SPLUMMMFFF!

But the glass bottle had a very soft landing.

*On my sticky-icky tum!*

"Saved by the *belly*," joked Isla.

## 22

# End Of The Ride

Now that the Big Wheel had come to a stop, the grounds of Tattiebogle Castle were filled with a brawsome silence.

Listen.

And a *not-so-brawsome*, bashed-up **FangFair**.
No more would the unfair funfair come to town –
unless Fangus was good at jigsaws and could stick
it all back together. (Hint: He wasn't!)

Aye, all was silent.

But not for long.

**OW-WOWW-WOWWW-WOWWWW!**

furry Fangus cried, as he took a ride down the
slide – with Nibbles on his tail. (*Really* on his tail!)

They walloped into the candyfloss machine and
sent us all tumbling and grumbling onto the ground.
I pawed at ma belly. The vile vial was gone!

*It's stuck to that tartan cat's tail!* wailed furry
Fangus. He crouched on four paws, ready to pounce.
*Give me that back!*

## 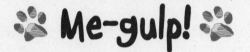 Me-gulp!

Luckily, another **TOTALLY** amazing and
**SLIGHTLY** unbelievable thing happened... The *Wee
Kiosk That Controlled The Ride* dropped from the sky.

# KRUMPPPP!

Fangus and Nibbles vanished from view. The kiosk door was wedged into the ground. They were 100% trapped, which was exactly the right amount.

"Caught like two spiders under a cup!" whooped Isla.

# 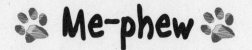 Me-phew

I wasn't ready to celebrate yet. A scarewolf was still holding Isla tight with both paws! Roaring Ross was still a scarewolf with claws!! And I still had to find dozy Dad somewhere outdoors!!!

I looked around for any sign of him, and that's when I spied with my little eye, Fangus's big wig on the ground. Something else was beside it. Something beginning with **W** and ending with **E**.

It wasn't a **whale**
or a **waffle**
or a **wardrobe**...

# 23

# Whistle

...It was a **WHISTLE**, of course. Good job I can speak 643 languages, including Dog-Whistle. Och, I'm sure I can do Scarewolf-Whistle. Here goes.

# Schweeeeeeeeeeeeeeeeeeeeeeeeep!

*Told you!*

I set Isla free, then commanded the scarewolves to come to me. Roaring Ross arrived first, wagging his tail. The others shuffled up, weary after such a long night of running around and standing still.

"Thank you, Porridge," Isla shouted, giving me a huge hug. She looked at Roaring Ross and the scarewolves. "We must find a way to turn them back into humans."

## 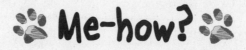 Me-how?

I meowed, padding around deep in thought and grass that needed cutting.

I accidentally tripped over Fangus's wig.

"That wig's fallen off his head," said Isla. "He's lost his silly curly locks."

Her words reminded me that Fangus had said the antidote was 'surrounded by locks' and 'out of reach!'... Maybe it had been hidden high up on his head? *Under his wig?*

## 🐾 Me-check 🐾

Now the wig was on the ground I could easily reach it. I stuck a curious paw inside lots of locks... and batted out a wee plastic bottle, full of a gloopy purple liquid!

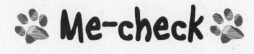

# 🐾 Me-yay! 🐾

"You've found it," gasped Isla. "Let's see what it says."

> *Take a sip to stop*
> *yourself being beastly!*
> *Aunty Dot*

"It's definitely Aunty Dot's antidote," she said, giving a glug to Roaring Ross and the other scarewolves.

She watched them all hopefully, but saw no sign of any change. "Maybe it's another of Fangus's tricks?"

*Or maybe it's taking longer, just to make the story more exciting?*

Nothing happened.

Then a bit more nothing happened.

Then suddenly all their scarewolf teeth and hair fell out!

PLINKLE- TINKLE 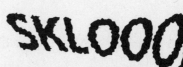 WHOMPFFF

Next, their sharp claws clattered to the ground and their scarewolf snouts sank out of sight.

CLANKLE- TANKLE SKLOOOP

Fourteen round black noses turned back to whatever shape they were before. All noses are different. Like carrots.

 SPLINGGGG

"What happened?" yawned Roaring Ross, as if waking up from a dream, except it was real life and he didn't have his pyjamas on. "Er, why do I have a tail?"

"Fangus changed you into a stinky scarewolf," explained Isla. "But Porridge found the antidote."

Roaring Ross suddenly coughed. And his tail fell off. Then it happened to the others too. (But not me.)

## 🐾 Me-phew 🐾

Now Ross was just an ordinary boy again, surrounded by ordinary fair-goers. They all chattered excitedly. None of them could really remember what had happened so they made up some stuff, such as zombie pirates and an alien spaceship. *And* a brave tartan cat – but that bit was true.

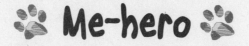

# Me-hero

Ross and the fair-goers were still picking wolf hair off their clothes when Dad strolled up. He had a sleepy look on his face. And a couple of cobwebs because he had been lying on the bench for so long.

"I had a wee nap," he yawned. "How long was I asleep?"

*About 126 pages.*

# 24

# In The Bag

Dad stared in astonishment at the broken, battered **FangFair**. Odd things were still dropping from the sky. One giant hammer. Three dodgem cars. Five chicken legs.

## Mmmm. Chicken.

I took a bite.

*Wax!*

"Did I miss anything?" asked Dad, a bit bewildered.

"Not much," replied Ross. "I became a scary wolf or something and found a pongy space rock in the loch."

"And Porridge and I stopped a plot to stink out the town by Fangus, the **FANGFAIR** owner," said Isla.

*And I'm going to write a book about how brawsome I was*, I meowed. Probably this one.

"What incredible imaginations you have," chuckled Dad. "Did you really find that long-lost space rock?"

I lifted ma tail and proudly presented the vile vial to Dad. He gave the bottle a wary sniff, then quickly popped it away in his bag.

"Mog-nificent!" he joked, doing his usual dodgy Dad dance. Then he gave us all a hug in the milky moonlight. I gave the milky moonlight a hopeful lick – but it wasn't milky at all – it tasted of moths.

## 🐾 Me-yuck! 🐾

"What's in the wee kiosk?" asked Dad... as it ran past us **ON SIX LEGS!!!**

"Just Fangus and Nibbles," giggled Isla.

The fair-goers chased after it, fed up with Fangus for ruining a funtastic funfair. We watched the wee

149

kiosk zigzag around the loch. As it vanished over
a distant hill, my *mega-super-well-OK-not-bad* ears
heard a catty voice say:

*Ow-woww-wowww-wowwww! Stop biting ma
bahookie! Sit. Heel. Lie Down!*

But Nibbles wouldn't Sit, Heel or Lie Down because she wasn't a daft dug. She was a big bad wolf who liked chasing cats. And she was delighted to have a happy ending in a storybook for a change.

But it wasn't quite the end for the twins and their tremendously terrific tartan cat (me again). You still have to read the final chapter of this book, where we find out what happened to the stinky space rock.

## 🐾 Me-whiff 🐾

# 25

# The Final Chapter Of This Book, Where We Find Out What Happened To The Stinky Space Rock

The next morning, we gave the stinky space rock to the director of the Tattiebogle Town Museum. Then everyone washed their hands. (It took me twice as long to wash ma paws.) She displayed the lump of **SPROUTINIUM** in a glass box, protected by laser beams so sensitive they probably cry at soppy movies.

## 🐾 Me-joke 🐾

Then we took Gran and Grandad home for lunch.

I thought we were getting **SEAFOOD SOUP!** Instead

Mum made us **SEE FOOD SOUP!**

"What's in it?" asked the twins.

"Everything I could see in the kitchen," said Mum, who loved experimenting. "Pasta and bananas and spinach and..."

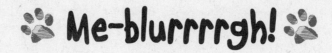

# Me-blurrrrgh!

(Och, it wasn't even fish-flavoured!)

Ross looked at himself in the back of his spoon. "On reflection, I'm glad I'm not a scarewolf any more," he said. "I had disgusting hair sprouting from my ears and my nose. Do you think Fangus will always be a mitten?"

"It depends if his Aunty Dot makes him another antidote," replied Isla.

"Well, I'm glad Fangus McFungus didn't manage to stink out the town," said Mum. "Scarewolves might have stolen all our precious things."

"My denarius coin," said Dad.

"My super-short shortbread recipe," said Mum.

"My football," said Ross.

"My goalie gloves," said Isla.

"My microphone," sang Gran.

"My brawsome bagpipes," tooted Grandad.

Hmmm. They all forgot to say the most precious thing of all.

My food bowl! (Full of fishy delishy biscuits, of course!)

## Me-yum-yum-yum-yum!

## I LOVE FISHY BISCUITS.

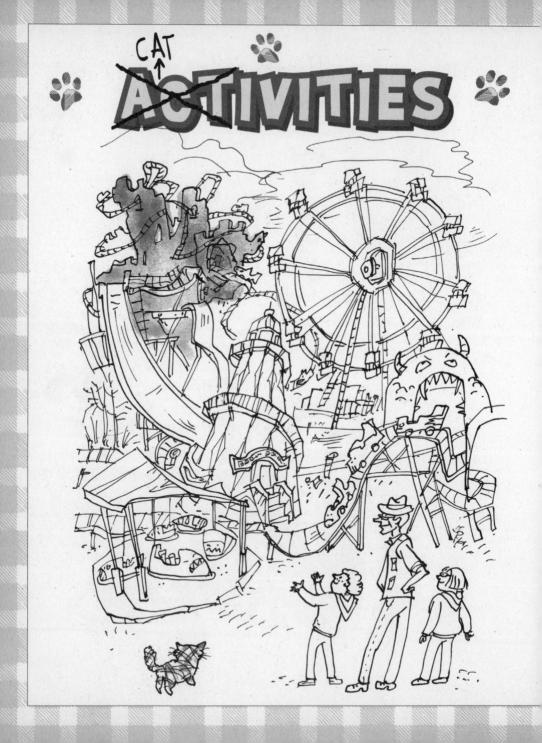

There are ten differences between these two pictures. Can you spot them all?